CAUGHT IN THE RAIN

by Beatriz Ferro
Illustrated by Robert Bigras

EARLY BIRD COLLECTION AUTHORS

John McInnes, *Senior Author*   Glen Dixon   John Ryckman

early bird

When you are caught out in the rain,
a tree can keep you dry,

and so can a broad mushroom,
if you are very small.

A wagon can keep you dry,

and so can a floppy hat.

A bridge will hide you from the rain
if you go underneath it.

The grocery awning blocks the rain,

and so does the morning paper.

Birds stay dry
in a hole in the wall,

or beneath a friendly statue.

You can be dry on a downtown bus,

or under Daddy's overcoat.

Even a boat upside down on the beach
will keep the rain away.

A tree,   a mushroom,   a wagon,

a hat,   a bridge,   an awning,

26

a paper,   a hole in the wall,   a statue,

a bus,   an overcoat,   a boat,

each of these is like a roof
that keeps you under cover.

But the very best way to get out of the rain
is by using an umbrella!

It's a portable roof
you can hold in your hand.
You can carry it anywhere.

It will keep you dry wherever you are,
when you get caught in the rain.

PUBLISHED SIMULTANEOUSLY IN 1990 BY:

Nelson Canada,
A Division of International
Thomson Limited
1120 Birchmount Road
Scarborough, Ontario   M1K 5G4

AND

Delmar Publishers Inc.,
A Division of Thomson Corp.
2 Computer Drive, West
Box 15015
Albany, NY 12212-5015

**Canadian Cataloguing
in Publication Data**

Ferro, Beatriz
   Caught in the rain

(Early bird collection)
Translation of: Per esempio un ombrello.
ISBN 0-17-603030-1

I. Bigras, Robert.   II. Title.   III. Series.

PZ7.F47Ca 1990   j853'.914   C89-090547-9

**Library of Congress
Cataloging-in-Publication Data**

Ferro, Beatriz.
   Caught in the rain.

(Early bird)
Translation of: Per esempio un ombrello.
   Summary: Depicts many ways to keep dry in the rain—
under a tree, a bridge, an awning, but best of all under an
umbrella.
   [1. Rain and rainfall—Fiction]. I. Title. II. Series: Early bird
(Albany, N.Y.)
PZ7.F418Cau   1989   [E]   89-23651
ISBN 0-8273-4128-8

Text copyright © 1978 by Emme Edizioni S.p.A.
Text originally published in 1978 in Italian, under the title
Per Esempio un Ombrello, by Emme Edizioni S.p.A.

Nelson Canada has make every attempt to trace the
ownership of copyright. Information that will enable the
publisher to rectify any error or omission will be welcomed.

Co-ordinating Editor: Jean Stinson
Project Manager: Jocelyn Van Huyse-Wilson
Editor: Irene Cox
Art Director: Lorraine Tuson
Series Design and Art Direction: Rob McPhail
Typesetting: Trigraph Inc.

1234567890 EB 9876543210